**Surf that wave! /**
Orange Back

145383

Ricci, Christine.

| WDC | | | |
|------|--|--|--|
|  | | | |
|  | | | |
|  | | | |
|  | | | |
|  | | | |
| J13 | | | |
| C1 | | | |
| CCS1 | | | |
| CCS | | | |

DEMCO

# Surf That Wave!

adapted by Christine Ricci
based on the teleplay by Janice Burgess and McPaul Smith
illustrated by Susan Hall

Ready-to-Read

SIMON SPOTLIGHT/NICK JR.
New York    London    Toronto    Sydney

Based on the TV series *Nick Jr. The Backyardigans*™ as seen on Nick Jr.®

SIMON SPOTLIGHT
An imprint of Simon & Schuster Children's Publishing Division
1230 Avenue of the Americas, New York, New York 10020
Manufactured in the United States of America
First Edition
2 4 6 8 10 9 7 5 3 1

Library of Congress Cataloging-in-Publication Data
Ricci, Christine.
Surf that wave! / by Christine Ricci ; illustrated by Susan Hall.-- 1st ed.
p. cm. -- (Ready-to-read)
"Based on the TV series Nick Jr. The Backyardigans as seen on Nick Jr."
ISBN-13: 978-1-4169-1482-2
ISBN-10: 1-4169-1482-X
I. Hall, Susan, 1940- II. Backyardigans (Television program) III. Title. IV. Series.
PZ7.R355Su 2006
[Fic]--dc22
2006004287

Hi! I am Pablo.

I am a surfer.

This is my surfboard.

I see a wave.

I paddle my surfboard.

I ride the wave!

# Watch this!

I can jump!

I can spin!

I can do a flip!

Oops!

# Wipeout!

I do it all over again!
I love surfing!